MONSTER ACADEMY FOR THE MAGICAL: THE MONSTER TRIAL

(MONSTER ACADEMY FOR THE MAGICAL, #3)

JESSICA SORENSEN

✽ Created with Vellum

HAVEN

*J*UDE HAS FOUND ME A SPONSOR.

Jude has found me a sponsor!

Yeah, that exclamation point is totally exaggerated, because I'm still not quite sure how I ended up with a sponsor. Harper seems a bit confused, too, so at least it's not just me.

"What do you mean someone anonymously sent her some money?" Harper questions.

Her, Jude, and I are sitting in the living room of my and Harper's dorm room. It's only been about half an hour since Roman left, after he showed me how to put my wings away. I can still feel the ache in my back, and my skin feels tight across my shoulder blades. I'm trying not to itch the area, since Harper was insistent that no one finds out that I'm part death angel and part maddening. Even Jude can't find out that I have wings hidden inside my body.

Wait ... Are they hidden inside my body? How does that even work?

"I mean exactly what I mean," Jude replies, drawing me from my thoughts. "That I received some money with a note that wasn't signed by anyone. But it did state that I was to give the money to Haven, and it arrived by portal mail."

"Portal mail?" I ask, wiggling my back a little, trying to stretch out my muscles without being too obvious.

"It means it appeared through a tiny portal invisible to the monster eye. Well, unless you're a mini pixie. They have crazy good eyesight," Harper explains to me then looks at Jude. "What else did the note say?"

Jude sticks his hand into his pocket and retrieves a piece of paper. "Here it is, if you want to look at it."

Harper takes the piece of paper from him. "They wrote it on paper. How old-school and very human-like."

"Even humans don't handwrite notes much

anymore," I inform her, scooting over to get a look at the note.

"Well, it's not just an ordinary piece of paper," Jude informs us, his hair smoking. "It was written with invisible ink on secret parchment."

I stare at them both blankly, again feeling completely and utterly confused. "What are those?"

Haven hands me the paper. "This is secret parchment, which means only creatures without malicious intent of the contents can see it. And invisible ink is … well, pretty much the same thing, only ink."

"Oh." I glance at the paper and am a bit relieved that I can see the writing on it. Before I can read all the details, though, it suddenly sizzles into ash.

"What the crap!" I exclaim, jumping to my feet as the ashes fall onto my lap.

Jude and Harper just chuckle.

"The secret parchment and ink also self-destructs once the note has served its purpose," Jude explains, rising to his feet. "The gist of it is that I'm to give the money to you." And yet, he makes no effort to hand me anything.

"Um … Okay. Where is it?" I wonder,

flicking a few stray pieces off the front of my jeans.

He smiles at me amusedly. "It's in your bank account."

"I don't have a bank account," I tell him then pause. "Wait. Monsters have banks?"

"Of course we have banks," Harper says, standing up. "Where else would we keep money?"

I shrug. "I don't know." Honestly, it seems weird they even use money at all when they all have magical powers.

"And to answer your first question," Jude says, reaching into his pocket and taking out a key. "I started a bank account for you." He hands it to me.

It's heavy, gold, and looks ancient, making me question what the hell it unlocks.

"You can use that to make any transaction you want," Jude tells me when he notes me just staring at the key. "Harper will be able to walk you through the process." He glances at her. "Right?"

Harper nods. "Of course. I've gotta go to a couple of stores, anyway, so I'll just take Haven with me and show her the ropes of shopping in the monster world."

"Thank you." Jude backs toward the door. "I have a meeting to run to, but I'll message you later to see how everything goes. I'm also going to look into who this sponsor is. I'll let you know if I find out anything. And please, *please* don't hesitate to call me if you need anything." He pauses in front of the door, gripping the doorknob, his fiery gaze bouncing between the two of us. "The both of you." He waits for Harper and me to nod then pulls the door open and walks out.

"Holy hell," Harper says, turning toward me. "I can't believe some random sponsor just sent you some money. This is crazy."

I nod like I know, but I don't. Not really. I mean, it seems crazy, but I feel like crazy in this world is a little different than the crazy that I'm used to.

"Did you see what the note said?" I wonder. "I didn't have enough time."

"All it said was that they were leaving you some money and that you were to use it for school." She wanders toward the kitchen. "And it was signed by *a friend*." She opens the fridge, takes out a bowl of strawberries, and starts munching on them. I'm noticing she does that a lot when she's stressed—stress eats strawberries. "It's so weird that the note just showed up, though. I mean, do you know who it could be from?"

I shake my head. "No. I don't even have any friends, so ..." I trail off as she looks at me with pity.

"I know that might've been true before, but you have friends now. You have me and Jules. And I'm sure you'll become friends with my friends."

Her and Jules are my friends?

God, I sound so stupid in my own head. Luckily, I'm keeping my thoughts tucked away inside my head ...

I mentally roll my eyes at myself. I sound crazy. Way to live up to my species.

Still, I manage a smile, hoping Harper doesn't have a clue that I'm having a conversation in my head with myself. She doesn't appear to notice, collecting the bowl off the counter and walking toward me.

"We should go shopping," she says, popping another strawberry into her mouth. "Buy you some supplies, new clothes, all things that are new."

I glance down at the key in my hand. "How do we even know how much money I have?"

Her eyes light up. "There are stations in a few of the foyers. We should go check."

I nod like I have a clue what she's talking about when I don't. At all. Still, I get up and follow her out of the room and into the hallway.

At the risk of looking stupid, I ask, "So, what's a station, anyway?"

"It's a place where you can check your account balance," she informs me, stuffing another strawberry into her mouth while hugging the bowl against her chest.

"So, like an ATM?"

"What's an ATM?"

"Um ... A machine in the human world where you can check your account balance and get cash and stuff."

She tilts her head to the side as she glances at me. "What's cash?"

"Um ..." I suddenly realize just how different the human world is from this one.

No, I take that back. I already realized that. I'm just realizing it more now.

"It's this paper stuff that humans use to pay

for the things they buy," I try to explain, taking a strawberry when she offers me one.

"Oh. Well, here we use coins, not paper." She pauses. "Are there coins in the human world?"

I nod, putting the strawberry in my mouth and trying not to moan at how delicious it tastes. But holy hell, it does.

How does food here taste so much better?

"We rarely take the coins out of the account, though," she explains, tapping the key I'm holding with her fingertip. "This is what you'll use to buy stuff. There will be machines in every store with a lock you can put it in when you're purchasing stuff."

"How does that work exactly? I mean, how does this key keep track of all the money I spend?" I turn over the key, examining it.

She smiles at me amusedly. "With magic."

"Oh, right." I clutch the key in my hand, feeling stupid.

She continues to smile at me. "Don't worry; you'll get the hang of everything. And if you ever get confused, the answer will almost always be related to magic."

I nod, making a mental note of that as we

come to a stop in an area where the hallway widens out into a large room. In the center of the room is a massive, padded bench that winds around a thick column that stretches up to a ceiling that is painted a glittery indigo, giving the illusion that water is above us.

So awesome.

Why is everything so awesome here?

Oh yeah, because of magic.

"Here we go." Harper skips up to a section of the wall that's covered in ancient-looking padlocks and stops in front of it. Then she turns to me and sticks out her free hand. "Let me see that key for a second." I hand it over to her, and she turns it over. "Let me see." She glances at the locks on the wall while chewing on her bottom lip. "Yep, I think …" She sticks the key into a large, bronzed lock that has a skeleton engraved into it. Once she gets the key in, she twists it and the padlock unlocks. Instead of removing it from the wall, though, she hands me back the key. "There you go. You have to ask it what your balance is since the key is spelled to only respond to your voice."

"Okay." I take the key from her and step

forward, putting the key in then staring at the unlocked lock. "Um ... What's my balance?"

The mouth of the engraved skeleton in front of the lock begins to move. "You're current balance is five hundred and fifty thousand monster coins," it says in a very deep voice.

While the number sounds like a lot, coins in the human world aren't that valuable anymore.

"So, what did it say?" Harper asks as I remove the key.

I twist to face her. "You didn't hear it?"

She shakes her head. "Nope. Only the account owner can hear the balance. Although, I have heard of spells that exist that allow some creatures to gain access to your account, so I'd recommend we get a magic box to keep the key in."

I don't ask what a magic box is, not wanting to give her question overload for the day.

"Okay." I pocket the key. "It said my balance was five hundred and fifty thousand monster coins."

Her eyes nearly bulge out of her head. "Are you being serious right now?"

I nod. "Why? Is that a lot?"

She gives an exaggerated nod. "That'll basically pay for all your schooling, clothes, supplies, and then some." She shakes her head in awe. "Man, whoever this friend is must really like you."

"I wonder who it is," I mutter as we wander back toward the room.

"I'm not sure, but Jules is looking into it, so maybe he'll find out." She sounds doubtful. "For now, I think you should enjoy the generosity of your sponsor and go shopping. We can go tomorrow morning. Get up bright and early, get some breakfast, and then spend the day buying a bunch of shit."

I can't help giggling at her word choice, but then confusion takes over. "Where do we go to shop?"

"Oh. We go to town." She loops her arm through mine. "You're so going to love it there. Plus, it'll be an excellent opportunity for you to learn more about this world. And you'll get to meet all sorts of crazy kinds of monsters."

I smile, pretending like I'm not scared out of my mind.

Meeting all sorts of crazy kinds of monsters? If that's not the thing of nightmares, I don't know what is.

ROMAN

I BARELY GET ANY SLEEP, MY HEAD FILLED
with all sorts of problems that I'm not sure how to
deal with. Mostly, my mind is stuck on the wing
match issue. I don't know what to do about it—
about the fact that my wing match is a maddening. I've spent years loathing them. My family
despises them. My brother is dead because of
one. And now, here I am, matched to one! We're
supposed to be soulmates. Yeah, fat chance of
that ever happening.

I know that's what's supposed to happen, but
there's no way I could ever fall in love with
Haven. Sure, she's gorgeous, but beneath that
beauty lies a monster. And besides, seeing a crea-

ture as beautiful doesn't mean you will fall in love. Trust me. My parents married each other on the basis that they both found each other pleasant to look at, and they can barely stand each other now.

Plus, just because she's my wing match doesn't mean I'm going to end up with her forever. Wing match magic can be broken. All magic can. I just need to find a way.

"Dude." Ollie's voice floats through the darkness of my bedroom. "You're thinking aloud again, and it's creepy."

I reach over and flip my lamp on. Then I sit up, blinking a few times until my eyes adjust to the sudden brightness and my vision comes into focus.

Ollie is standing in the doorway, dressed head to toe in black, including a pair of black gloves and a knit cap.

"And you're creeping around in the dark again, which is creepy," I mutter tiredly then sigh. "Where are you going?"

He shrugs, leaning against the wall with his arms crossed. "Out. I'd elaborate more, but I feel like the less you know about what I'm doing, the better. That way, if I get caught, you can just say you didn't know what I was doing."

I arch a brow. "Since when do we care if we get in trouble? Besides, even if you told me, I'd just lie anyway."

"True." He wavers. "But, considering you're our key to winning the games this year, I think it might be better if we keep you out of trouble."

I give him an unimpressed look. "First of all, I'm not the key to winning it. Just because I found my ... wing match"—I frown, those worried thoughts that were haunting my mind just moments ago returning—"doesn't mean I'm going to have enough power to win now. And second, since when do you, and I'm assuming Phoenix, make decisions without me being part of it?"

"Well, normally, we don't, but mostly because you decided the day we formed our group that you were going to be the leader. And, might I add, you made that decision without Phoenix and me." He straightens. "And we've always been okay with that. Phoenix and I would be terrible leaders, considering I'm flaky as hell and Phoenix is completely irrational most days." He wavers, rubbing his lips together. "However, for the time being, you need to focus on the games and strengthening your powers with our new secret weapon."

"You mean the maddening?" I mutter grumpily.

He sighs. "Dude, look, I get your issues with this—I really do. However, if you want this to work, you're going to have to at least develop somewhat of a relationship with her. Or, at least pretend to, which means you should probably start calling her by her name instead of maddening." He glances at his watch as it dings. "Shit, I'm running late." He looks up at me again. "But think about what I said, okay?" He doesn't wait for me to reply, simply hurrying off toward the front door. Then he leaves the dorm.

I check the time, and my confusion doubles. It's just after two o'clock in the morning. Where the hell is he going? And why is he all decked out in black? The only reason I can think of is that he wants to blend in with the night without using magic. Again: why?

I could ask Phoenix but, more than likely, he's out at a feeding bar or something—vampires are night bats like that. Still, I get up and check his bedroom just to make sure he's not there. His bed is empty, of course, so I head back to my room and climb into bed.

I feel way too awake right now to lie down, so I start pacing the room, restless energy bursting inside me. I'm irritated, upset, annoyed, and nervous about tomorrow, which I hate.

I used to get nervous all the time when I was younger. But that was back when I was nice. Back when I was weak. I'm no longer that creature anymore, something the scars on my arms remind me of. Still, even when I look at the white lines covering my flesh, I can't calm down. They remind me too much of what happened. What my father did to me.

"I need to get the hell out of here," I mutter as I stride toward my closet.

I grab a pair of boots, strip my shirt off, then leave the dorm, heading straight up to the rooftop. Technically, I'm not supposed to fly at night—it's an academy rule—but I've never been much for rules. So, taking a deep breath, I let my wings snap out of my back and, as the feathers spread behind me, some of that tension releases from my body.

I step up onto the ledge and stare down at the tree-covered land, at the stars and moons in the sky reflecting across the silvery grass. In the distance, the city shines like its own star.

This land really is beautiful to look at, but I know firsthand of the dangers hiding in the darkness, especially at night when all the real monsters come out. That doesn't stop me from leaping off the ledge.

The instant the wind hits my wings, contentment fills my body as I soar through the sky and over the trees. I'm not sure where I'm going or if I'm really going anywhere; I just needed to get out to clear my head. And, with each flap of my wings, more and more tension evaporates from my body.

Eventually, I decide to take a break and land in one of the trees, on a branch high enough that I can almost reach the stars. I sit down and simply stare up at the sky, remembering what it was like when I was younger and actually believed I could grab the stars. My brother was the one who told me it wasn't possible, that the stars in our world were nothing but an illusion created by magic.

"Really?" I ask him in disappointment.

We are lying in the grass with our wings out, relaxing after a long flight. He has been trying to teach me how to nosedive without crashing into the ground. However, I failed enough times that my face hurts. He never gives up on me, though, and says we'll keep practicing until I get it right.

I like when he teaches me things. It's easier with him than when our father tries to teach me. He always gets so frustrated with me.

"Yeah, sorry, bud." He reaches over and ruffles my hair. "There are worlds that have real stars. They're mainly just fire, so you still can't grab them."

"That sucks," I say with a heavy sigh. "Is there anything in the sky that you can touch?"

He tucks his arms under his head. "I've heard stories about creatures hiding things up there, but I'm not sure how much truth there is to it."

I glance at him. "What sort of things?"

"Powerful things." He shrugs. "I heard a story once about a powerful genie who hid his lamp up there so no one could find it. I'm not sure if there's truth to it. And some creatures believe that our souls get hidden up there when we die."

"Really?" I return my gaze to the sky, looking for these souls. "What does a soul look like?"

He shrugs again. "I'm not sure." Then he

cracks a smile as he looks at me. "When I die, I'll let you know."

He meant it as a joke, but I panic at the idea of losing him. He is the only one in my family who isn't angry all the time, like our father who carries so much rage that it constantly rumbles through our home. And our mom who sits in her quiet anger that releases an unsettling and uncomfortable silence that seeps and pollutes the air. I honestly hate being in our house. If I had my way, I'd just stay outside and hang out with my brother all the time.

"Don't ever die," I whisper, panicking.

He just smiles. "Don't worry; it won't happen for a while."

That had been a lie, since he died a few years later. Because he was too nice and let a maddening into his life. Just like I'm supposed to now.

Just like that, all the emotions I flew away from return full force.

I don't want to get to know Haven, whether it be pretend or not. But, if I don't, I'll be reducing my chances of winning the deadly games, which means I'll be reducing my chances of bringing my brother back from the dead.

I can do this, I tell myself. *For him, I can pretend to like her.*

I sit in the tree for a while, telling myself that over and over again until the illusion of the stars melts away as the suns rise in the east and the north; one silver, one lavender. The light collides in the middle of the sky, making everything appear grey.

I get to my feet, preparing to take flight and fly back to the castle, then pause when I spot something in the trees below me. I crouch down and squint, trying to get a better look, but the shadows are too deep down there, so I tilt my head and listen.

"What took you so long?" a female hisses.

I know that voice.

Sage.

Why is she out here in the forest? And who is she talking to?

I lean forward and peer around the midnight blue leaves that cover the branches. At first, I don't see anyone and wonder if she's just talking to herself. Then a figure steps out from the trees. I can't see their face, though.

"Do not take that tone with me." The cold, clipped tone sends a shiver down my spine.

What in the hell is my father doing here? Better yet, why is he creeping around in the forest and meeting up with Sage?

"I'm so sorry." Sage, who is one of the biggest bitches I've ever met and who basically controls Mor, suddenly turns into some sort of reserved, timid creature.

"That's much better." My father peers around. "Are you sure you weren't followed?"

At that, I hunker down lower and tuck my wings tight against my back, hoping the leaves are blocking me from their view.

"Of course I'm sure," Sage says assuredly. "I slipped a sleeping poppy into Mor's drink before I left. He won't be awake for hours."

"Good. Then let's go."

When they grow quiet, I peek through the branches, trying to see where they're going, and catch sight of them slipping through an open portal that closes up right behind them.

An unsettling feeling stirs inside my stomach. When my father is involved in things, it's generally for bad reasons. Maybe he's just sleeping with Sage. After all, he's had a lot of affairs during his marriage with my mom—both of my parents have. But it didn't feel like that.

And why take a portal somewhere? They're very magic costly.

And I can't help thinking how involved Sage is with the academy now.

More than likely, they're up to something.

And if they are, I need to find out what.

ROMAN

After seeing the whole thing with Sage and my father, I fly back to the academy and head back to my room, hoping Ollie and Phoenix are there so I can tell them what happened.

When I enter the dorm, Phoenix is lounging on one of the sofas with his shoes kicked off and his lips stained red, either from the blood he drank last night or the blood berries he's currently eating. He also has his handheld out and is reading something on it.

"Did you know that over a hundred maddenings were killed three years ago," he says as he swipes his finger across the screen. "But two years ago, that number dropped by half. And last year, only twenty were killed."

I close the door behind me. "Okay, why the hell are you telling me facts about how many maddenings were killed?"

He lowers his feet to the floor and sits up, looking at me with amusement—Phoenix almost always looks amused. "I'm telling you this because the reason behind the decline in maddening killings is because of the decrease in their species' population." He sets the handheld down on the table and sits back with his hands tucked behind his head. "They're almost extinct, yet somehow a hybrid one ended up being your wing match." He bites back a grin. "Out of all the creatures walking around, that's what Destiny decided to do to it. It's like she fucking hates you."

I narrow my eyes at him. "This isn't funny. And Destiny isn't a she. It's an essence, which has no gender or species. Well, or it could be all of them, depending on how you want to look at it."

He rolls his eyes. "Thank you for reciting Intro to Destiny 101."

I start across the room, heading toward the kitchen to get something to eat and drink. Flying always makes me hungry and thirsty. "You're the one who started giving me facts about maddenings. I'm just returning the favor."

"I'm giving you these facts for a reason." He rises to his feet and wanders into the kitchen after me. "I know you hate their kind and for a totally justifiable reason, but in order for this to work, you're going to have to learn more about them." He rests his arms on top of the island counter. "And you're going to have to learn more about her."

Shaking my head, I jerk open the fridge. "You and Ollie are really starting to piss me off with your pathetic attempts at trying to boss me around."

"No one's trying to boss you around," he assures. "We just both know that this is going to be complicated for you. But, despite those complications, this has to work."

He's being serious, which he rarely is. This is different, though. We all want to win the games and the crown for our own reasons—to bring back our lost loved ones. I think Phoenix might have a deeper reason. I just haven't figured out what yet, and he always denies it whenever I ask him. I can sense it, though, every time the games are mentioned.

"I know that." I grab some berry juice, twist the cap off, and take a swig. If my mom saw me doing this, she'd scream a fifteen minute lecture at me then make me drink the entire thing as a punishment. It's one of the many reasons I prefer being here at the academy and why I come here earlier than most of the students—it lets me escape the hellhole that is my house.

Well, it's not literally a hellhole. Those only exist in the Underworld, but you get the picture.

"And to ease yours and Ollie's minds, I'm going to head over to the madden—Haven's dorm room this morning." I put the juice back in the fridge.

"Good." He takes out a bag of crispy bat wings and starts munching on them. "Are you still going to make that blood promise with Harper?"

I open a cupboard. "I have to or she won't let me see Haven."

The corners of his lips quirk upward. "*Let you*, huh?"

I grab a bag of cookies. "If she wasn't Ollie's twin sister, I wouldn't have agreed to it. But I'm not about to go after her to get out of a blood promise that I'll follow through with anyway."

Because I'm not going to hurt Haven. Only because I need her to win the games.

"True. Although, I'm not thrilled you agreed to bring her into our group."

"I didn't agree to that. I agreed to *pretend* she was in our group. It's all for appearance and nothing more."

"Yeah, but that means we're going to have to have her back if she gets in trouble, which, considering she doesn't seem to know shit about our world, she'll probably get in trouble a lot."

"I know that. And I know it sucks, but we need to do this if we want to win the games."

"Yeah, maybe." He pops another crispy bat wing into his mouth. "Do you know Ollie snuck out somewhere last night? He's not even back yet, which is weird for him."

"I know. I saw him before he took off. He was all decked out in black, so I'm guessing he was going somewhere he didn't want to be seen but didn't want to use his magic either."

"Weird." He gives a short pause. "Don't you think he's been acting kind of strange over the last few weeks?"

I lift a shoulder as I open the bag of cookies. "It's probably because he's been at home for the summer ... You know how he gets when he's at that house for too long." House is an understatement. Ollie's home is more like a prison. In fact, the house his family resides in has a cage in it. I once asked him about it when I was hanging out there, and he just shrugged and turned very pale.

Phoenix dazes off as he stuffs another bat wing into his mouth. "I'm going to ask him where he went when he gets back."

"Good luck with that. He seemed really reluctant to tell me anything. Although, he said that was because you and him decided that I just needed to focus on Haven and nothing else, and that you two were going to take care of everything else?" I cock a brow in insinuation.

He gives a shrug. "Sorry, but it needs to happen. You can't train a clueless maddening/death angel to win the fucking deadly games and take care of all the other stuff we have going on. You'll start to crack. And cracks lead to weakness. And we can't have that."

"I get what you're saying, but you guys didn't have to talk about this behind my back."

"We kind of did, though." He opens the cupboard and puts the bag of bat wings back inside it. "If we had talked about it with you, you would've tried to talk us out of it.

"I still might anyway."

He turns to face me, leaning back against the counter with his arms crossed and amusement tugging at his lips. "Yeah, but this way, Ollie and I formed a coalition."

"Against me?" I question flatly.

"Kind of." He pats me on the shoulder. "It's nothing personal. We just need to win the games and this—having you focus on Haven and strengthening your power with her—is going to help big time."

Deep down, I know he's right. That doesn't make any of this easier. Doesn't make the fact that my wing match is half-maddening. And why is she even half-maddening? Hybrids are even rarer than maddenings. And a hybrid maddening ... Yeah, that's pretty unheard of. Not to mention, she probably could be extremely powerful if she had the right training. Not that I'm going to train her to become more powerful than me. That's the last thing I want. She does need to be powerful enough for the games, though. And powerful enough to protect herself, because her being a maddening and a hybrid puts her in danger of power-hungry creatures, which means no one else can know about her. I don't even like that Jude, Mor, and Sage know about her ...

Speaking of which ...

"So, while I was out flying, I saw something weird and potentially concerning," I inform Phoenix as I grab a few cookies then return the bag to the cupboard.

He pauses in the doorway and turns back toward me. "Really?"

I nod then give him a recap of what I saw and heard.

"A portal?" he asks after I'm done. "But your father can't open portals himself."

"I know, but he's very good at persuading creatures to do stuff for him," I mumble. "He's always been an excellent manipulator."

"True." He pauses. "But, where would they be going to through a portal? And what in the hell is he doing with bitchy Sage?"

I nibble on the corner of a cookie. "That's what I'd like to know, too."

He considers something. "Ollie and I'll look into it. You focus on Haven."

I want to argue with him for several different reasons, but the truth is that I'm weak when it comes to my father, so it's better if Ollie and Phoenix look into it.

Once we agree to a plan, I head to take a shower. Then I put on a pair of jeans, a black shirt, and pair of boots before collecting my dagger from my weapons collection that I keep hidden in a trap door in my closet. Ollie and Phoenix have one, too.

We don't use weapons often, but there have been a handful of situations where they've been useful. Right now, I'm simply bringing the dagger so I can make the blood promise with Harper, something I'm not thrilled about. But, like I told Phoenix, it's not like I'm going to let Haven get hurt anyway, since she's going to help us win the games.

The academy is quiet as I make my way through the halls. In a few days, though, the place will be packed.

I hate crowds. Not that I'll ever let that on. Letting people get to know you means allowing them to see the cracks in your armor. And my armor is what keeps me safe. Letting anyone see what's beneath it—see the real me—means giving someone a chance to use the information against me. Not even Ollie and Phoenix know everything about me, though they know more than any other creature. Well, except for my brother. He knew the real me. Realness doesn't exist anymore. Everything I do has a motive. Like helping Haven right now.

I slow to a stop as I reach their dorm. Then I tuck my dagger in my back pocket before knocking, knowing Harper will flip out if she sees it. I just get it put away when the door is opened.

Harper's eyes widen slightly when she sees me, but then she narrows her gaze at me. "What're you doing here?"

Is she being serious? "Did you hit your head? Or accidentally cast a forget spell on yourself ... again?"

She holds up a finger. "That happened one time, and that was way, way back before I became the awesome skilled faerie that I am now." She flashes me a snarky grin before growing cold again. "Seriously, why are you here?"

I shake my head. "To do the blood promise so I can get started on helping Haven learn how to control her powers. You know, something we agreed to do just yesterday."

She crosses her arms. "Yeah, I know, but I honestly thought you'd blow this off."

"Why? I already told you I need her for the games."

"True, but still." She rubs her lips together, studying me. "I've known you for a long time, Roman, and the fact that you're here has me very suspicious."

I roll my eyes but don't argue since she really does have a reason to be suspicious. I'm not trustworthy, and I don't really care if I am. All I care about is that me, Ollie, and Phoenix are safe. That's it.

"Well, the blood promise we're going to do should alleviate your suspicions," I inform her. "So, how about we get that done so we can move past this annoying conversation?"

Her lips twitch in annoyance, but she steps back and gestures for me to come in.

The moment I step over the threshold, I can smell *her*. And I'm not talking about Harper. No, I can smell the scent of something sweet and sugary, like spun sugar, and somehow I just know

...

That's Haven's scent.

The revelation sends annoyance biting

through my veins. This has to be a wing match thing, which has me worried about what else is going to happen because of it. I don't like that I'm in unknown territory.

While I know a lot about wing matches, I don't know everything, so I make a mental note to look into it some more.

Once Harper closes the door, she turns around and looks at me. "You look like shit."

"So do you."

"Hardy, har, har, Roman. You're such an ass." Shaking her head, she steps toward me. "I just mean you look like tired."

I shrug, stuffing my hands into my pockets. "I didn't sleep for very long."

She smiles at me sweetly. "Aw, did the poor death angel have a bad dream last night?" Her grin turns wicked. "I remember, whenever you had sleepovers with Ollie, you'd wake up screaming in the middle of the night, scared out of your damn mind. But that was back when you could still feel stuff. I didn't realize this asshole, robotic version of you felt much of anything."

I stab my fingernails into my palms as I feel the shadows of darkness rising across my skin. "Careful," I warn. "Or this robotic asshole might decide to hell with the fact that you're Ollie's sister."

Her brow curves upward. "Wow, is that a threat?" she mocks then pats me on the head. "Hate to break it to you, death angel, but I know you won't hurt me. You may hate almost every creature, but Ollie and Phoenix are your kryptonite." She muses over something. "Well, and I guess Haven is now, too."

The muscles in my jaw pulsate. "Just because she's my wing match, doesn't mean I care about her."

"Yeah, so? It means you'll protect her, and that's enough."

"And yet, you're making me do a blood promise to make sure of something you seem so confident about."

"What can I say? I like the fact that I get to make you do things you don't want to do. It makes me feel powerful." She smirks. "Plus, despite my confidence, I do have a tiny bit of doubt that perhaps even the ancient wing match magic might not be strong enough to go against your sadistic tendencies."

"My sadistic tendencies?" I question, lifting a brow. "You're the one getting off on this."

"Perhaps, but that doesn't make me a sadist. You, however, have gotten off several times on making other people suffer. Like, for instance, the other day when you locked Haven in a cage. And then when you took her to the cave."

"I didn't get off on that. I thought I was doing everyone a favor by getting rid of a maddening." My lips kick up into a taunting smirk. "You know, those creatures that everyone fears because they love to kill." The words burn my tongue. The truth burns my tongue.

Maddenings are killers, and I'm wing matched to one. Destiny must loathe me. Not that I believe I deserve better.

She taps her finger against her lips. "You know, I think I read once somewhere that death angels get wing matched to creatures they're compatible with."

"I'm nothing like a maddening," I growl out, the shadows inside me begging to be let out, begging to curse her. Not that I'm going to. But I figure I can at least spook her with the idea that I might.

"You should be so lucky as to be like Haven." She jabs me in the chest with her fingertip, apparently unafraid of my shadows. "She's one of the nicest creatures I've ever met. A little broken perhaps, but aren't we all?"

Whether she meant that personally, I haven't got a damn clue, but I take it as a jab at me. Harper knows me well enough that she's seen all my sides—the good, shattered, weak, bad, and broken. And I hate that she has.

"You've known her for only a handful of days; that's not enough time to know who a creature is," I say in the calmest tone I can muster. "It takes years to get to know someone, and even then, you can't completely trust anyone."

She shakes her head, strands of hair falling into her eyes that are filled with something that both makes me cringe and pisses me off.

"I feel sorry for you. I really do," she says.

I'm about to insult her in every way possible when her handheld goes off.

"Crap." She rushes over to the table, collects it, and then reads the message she just received. "Dammit. One of the professors that I'm assisting wants to meet up this morning to go over what I'll be doing."

"So go," I tell her, unsure what the big deal is. "It only takes a couple of minutes to do a blood promise. You should know that by now."

"I do know that." She stares at the screen of the handheld while chewing on her bottom lip. "I'm not worried about how long that'll take. I just told Haven I'd take her shopping this morning."

"She got a sponsor then, I take it."

She nods, setting the handheld down. "That's why Jude stopped by last night."

"Who is her sponsor?" I wonder, curious as to who in the hell mouth demons Jude managed to wrangle into sponsoring a monster from the human world who just found out she was a monster.

Although, maybe he lied about her backstory. Probably. In fact, I hope he did, because the less creatures that know the truth about the half-maddening, the less of a chance others will find out. And that's what I need ... for right now.

Harper gives a half-shrug. "I have no idea. Jude said the money was donated to Haven anonymously."

"Really?" I question. "That sounds suspicious."

"It does a little bit," she agrees. "What's even weirder is how much money they donated."

"How much was it?"

"Now, why would I tell you?"

I snort a laugh. "What? You think I'm going to try to rob her because I'm so hard up for money?"

She dramatically rolls her eyes. "You sound like an entitled, spoiled brat."

"Almost every monster who goes here is an entitled, spoiled brat," I point out. "Including you."

"I'm not denying what I am. But not every monster here is entitled or a brat." She gives a pressing look at one of the bedroom doorways; I'm assuming the one that leads to Haven's room.

While I'm not a fan of maddenings, she's definitely right about this. From the file I read on Haven, she grew up in foster homes and showed up here with everything she owns, which can fit in a backpack. The old me may have felt sorry for her, and maybe I do a little bit, but then I think of my brother, who felt sorry for a maddening once and look at where it got him.

As Harper's handheld goes off again, she grimaces. "Crap, I'm going to have to cancel the shopping trip with Haven. I feel bad. Plus, after today, students are going to start showing up, and it's better if she has all new things by then."

By new students, she probably means their roommates, aka her friends, which the death triplets used to refer to as the bitch squad.

While Harper can get on my nerves sometimes, she's never been cruel to others. Her friends, though, are nothing like her. Not that I'm one to judge, but Harper has always been blind when it comes to friends. She can't see them for what they really are. I think it's because she used to be bullied when we were younger. Ollie, Phoenix, and I tried to protect her, but we weren't as powerful as we are now. Plus, Harper was stubborn and insisted she didn't need our help.

She still is really stubborn.

"It's probably better if she doesn't go shopping this morning, anyway. Since, you know, I'm supposed to be starting to train her," I remind her, my tone oozing with sarcasm.

Her gaze flits to me, and her eyes start to narrow, but then she hesitates, contemplation flickering in her eyes. "Actually, I may have an idea that can fix the problem. I just need to decide if I trust you."

Irritation prickles through me. "How many times do I have to tell you that this blood promise is going to alleviate that distrust?" I reach around and grab the dagger out from my back pocket. "So, how about we get it done so you can stop sounding like a broken magic spell."

She considers for a while; I think dragging it on purpose to annoy me. "Fine. Let's do it." She sticks out her hand. "But be careful with your word choice."

"Obviously." I resist an eye roll.

Like I'm not going to be careful with what we're promising. When it comes to making blood promises, you need to be careful with your wording or you could end up promising something you don't mean to.

Once I slice my palm open with the tip of the dagger, I hand it to Harper. While she's cutting her palm open, I go over in my head what I should promise. I want to be careful enough that if I need to take Haven down, I still can. Like, if she tries to use her powers against me, Ollie, and Phoenix. But I also need to make sure Harper is satisfied with my wording, as well.

"Ready?" she asks as blood trickles out of her wound.

Nodding, I press my palm against hers and utter, *"Dummodo illa ad portum laedere sic iuravi ut non nocuerunt dosn't necesse alia creatura. Promitto et auxilium eius uti ad eius potestatem.*" I look at Harper. "Does that work?"

She wavers. "I'm not a huge fan about the *if she hurts another creature unnecessarily* you can still hurt her."

I shake my head. "I'm not going to promise never to hurt her when I know nothing about her, except that she's part maddening and part death angel."

She scowls at me. "She would never hurt anyone, Roman."

"If you know that, then this shouldn't be a problem."

She hesitates then nods. "You're right." Then she utters the promise like I did, and the faint sizzle of blood promise magic crackles through us.

Once it's all done, I lower my hand from Harper's. "There. Now you can trust me."

She snorts a laugh. "Yeah, I'll never fully trust you, but I trust you not to hurt Haven." She moves over to the kitchen, grabs a dish towel, and presses it against the wound on her hand.

I wander over to kitchen, too, turn on the sink, and wash the blood off my hand. "I think I'll take her to the training room this morning. As soon as other students start showing up, I'm probably going to have to find another place to train her. I also think it might be a good idea to tell everyone she's just a death angel instead of a firelight witch. It wouldn't make sense for us to bring her into our group if she was one. Plus, it might be better for her to pretend to be one of the creatures she actually is. That way she can learn about stuff that'll help her."

She sets the towel down. "Don't you think that might be risky?"

"It's only risky if anyone finds out she's a hybrid," I say, picking up a towel to dry off my hand.

"Mor, Sage, and Jude all know that she's a maddening," she stresses. "So, if we tell them she's also a death angel, then they'll know she's a hybrid. And, while I'm pretty sure Jude is trustworthy, Mor is definitely iffy. And Sage—"

"Sage definitely isn't," I cut her off, realizing… "You're right. We'll stick to the firelight witch story."

She eyes me over warily. "Did you just admit I'm right? What in the crazy bats is wrong with you?"

"Nothing's wrong with me." I stick my dagger underneath the faucet to clean the blood off the blade. "I just agree with you on this."

Her gaze bores into me. "You know something."

"I know a lot of things." I could tell her about Sage and my father's secret rendezvous in the forest, but I'm not going to. Until I figure out what's going on between the two of them, I'm not going to tell anyone besides Ollie and Phoenix. But I do need to make sure Harper understands ... "Just be careful around Sage, okay?" I turn off the faucet. "I don't trust her. And she has a lot of control over Mor, so I don't trust him, either." I'm still a bit skeptical about Jude, too, but Harper likes Jude, and if I bring him up, it'll only lead to another argument. I'm done with those for the morning. At least, I think so, but then Harper has to go and open her mouth again.

"Fine. I'll be careful around them. And I'll make sure Haven is, too, whenever I'm around her." She rests her arms on the counter and smiles at me sweetly. "However, you're going to have to keep an eye on her this morning when you take her shopping."

I give her an appalled look. "I so am fucking not taking her shopping."

"Um, you so fucking are," she mimics my tone. "She needs to go shopping, and now that I have that promise that I can trust you, I think you can take her this morning since I can't."

"I never agreed to a shopping trip," I say flatly.

"So? You don't want anyone to be suspicious of her and try to dig into her past, right? Which means she needs to blend in and be as inconspicuous as possible." She gives me a pressing look. "Right now, with the stuff she owns, she looks like a human. Plus, she doesn't have any supplies, which is going to seem odd."

She has a point, a very annoying point, but there is one other small problem about what she's saying.

I dry off my dagger with a towel. "Even if we get her clothes and supplies to help her blend in, she's still going to stand out."

"And why's that?"

"Well, for starters, she's going to be pretending to be part of my group, so she'll draw attention from that." That's not the only reason. I just don't want to say the other one aloud.

Her eyes glitter with amusement, as if she knows exactly what I'm thinking. "Is that the only reason?"

"Does it matter if it isn't? It's a valid enough reason."

She smirks. "I know, but I want to hear you say the other one aloud."

I roll my eyes. She can be so damn annoying sometimes.

"Fine, I'll say it. She's gorgeous, and that's going to draw attention." I give a shrug, like I didn't just compliment a maddening. A maddening that's my wing match and who I'm going to take shopping today.

My lip twitches in annoyance. I want to back out of this now. But it doesn't really matter how annoyed I am. I can't back out of this. Not if I want a chance at winning that crown.

Harper starts to wander off to go get ready to meet her professor when I suggest waking Haven, but she tells me not to, that I need to let her rest because she could hear Haven up half the damn night, tossing and turning and moaning.

"Moaning?" I have to ask.

"I think she was having a nightmare," Harper explains. "I think she has them every night, too."

"I wonder what that's about." As soon as the words pass my lips, I want to retract them.

Since when do I worry about maddenings?

"Aw, your wing match tendencies are showing," Harper mocks with a smirk.

When I narrow my eyes at her, my lips parting with an asshole-ish remark, she just laughs at me and skips out of the room.

I shake my head, settling back on the sofa, restlessness bursting through me. Although, I'm not sure if it's mine. It feels like it might be coming from something else, which is strange.

I glance at Haven's bedroom doorway with the most overwhelming urge to go lie down beside her and comfort her. I think the restlessness might be floating from her. It's annoying as hell. I was fine this morning when I was in my dorm. Now that I'm close to her, with her scent engulfing me ...

I ball my hands into fists. This isn't good. At all. The last thing I need is to be craving to touch a maddening, to get close to her. What I need is to look up information about wing matches and see what I can find out. See if I can find a way to shut off this connection stirring inside me.

Since I have a ton of books back in my room, I message Phoenix to look through them and see if he can find anything useful that will allow me to not bond further with the maddening. It takes him a bit, but he does message me back, informing me that he didn't find a way yet, but that he did stumble upon something interesting.

Apparently, wing match magic allows wing matches to feel each other's emotions. It also helps you detect when the other is lying, which means, if I want to, I can find out all the maddening's secrets.

"I think it's time to give her a little monster trail test," Phoenix says through the handheld.

"I completely agree," I tell him.

Yeah, it's definitely time to give the maddening a little test, use this wing-match power to find out the truth. Find out just how much of a monster she is, something I've wanted to do from the moment I found out what she is.

HAVEN

I can hear the soft murmuring of voices as I hover somewhere in the borders of dreamland, not quite awake, but not fully asleep. I try to wake up, but I'm exhausted from the nightmares I had last night. Some were of my past, while others were of me sitting in the middle of a pit of fire, the flames burning my wings away. So, yeah, basically, I slept like shit.

It takes me a while to get my eyes open, and by the time I do, the voices have quieted, making me question if I imagined them.

It takes me another moment to get my brain fully turned on, and then yesterday's events come rushing back to me.

I have wings.

I am a death angel.

And a maddening.

I'm a monster.

I blow out a breath as I sit up and rub my eyes, trying not to focus on that fact. Otherwise, I might sink into a pit of depression. So, instead, I focus on the shopping trip that I'm going on with Harper.

While I'm not a huge fan of shopping, I'm kind of excited to be leaving the academy and endeavoring into the city. I'm also scared.

I'm not sure what a monster city looks like. In my head, it's all kinds of wicked scariness. Like, when I was younger and I used to imagine that this big, hairy, three-eyed monster with fangs as sharp as knives and claws covering its beastly hands and feet lived in my closet. That's what I imagine the town filled with and, honestly, I could be right. I also realize that maybe the monster I thought I had imagined living in my closet could have been real ...

I shiver at the thought as I climb out of bed, grab a pair of black jeans and a grey shirt, then head into the bathroom to take a shower and get dressed up. As I move, I notice that thankfully, the aching and itchiness in my back that I had felt yesterday has subsided.

The dorm is quiet. Like, super quiet. So much so that I wonder if Harper went somewhere and I'm here alone. But, as I'm exiting my room, I become aware that I'm not alone, and that I'm not alone with the last creature I ever want to be alone with, which is a really weird way to say that …

I grind to a halt and put my guard up.

"What're you doing here?" I ask Roman, hugging my clothes against my chest.

"Waiting for you to wake up," he says without glancing up at me. He's sitting on the sofa, staring at his handheld device.

"What? Why?"

He lifts his gaze, and the moment his shadowy eyes land on me, I feel this weird pull, like a string is attached to my heart and he just yanked on it.

What in the hell?

"Because I'm taking you shopping today," he answers with indifference.

I allow a slow breath to ease from my lips before saying, "No. No way. I'm going with Harper." I take a step back as he stands up.

He's dressed in a black shirt with the sleeves rolled up, grey jeans, and has a pocket watch dangling from his pocket. Leather bands cover his wrists, and the metal piercings in his face glint in the low lighting of the chandelier.

"Nope. There's been a change of plans. You're going with me." He stretches his long legs as he takes a step toward me.

I take another step back, even though that pull is begging me to step forward. "No, I'm not. And how did you even find out I was going shopping? And where the heck is Harper?" I peer around the room, as if expecting her to materialize from out of thin air.

Of course, she doesn't. Not that she can't.

"I found out because Harper told me after I showed up here to finish the blood promise we agreed to yesterday." He crosses his arms and stares at me with an indecipherable look on his face. "You're supposed to start training with me today. However, Harper had to go meet with a professor this morning, so we agreed that I would take you shopping. And while we shop, I can teach you some stuff."

My lips tug downward. "And neither of you thought to ask me how I felt about this?"

He assesses me, like he's trying to put together a complex puzzle. "Harper wanted to, and probably would've, but she got distracted by other stuff."

I'm unsure if I trust him. Sure, he helped me get my wings put away yesterday, but he also tried to do a lot of other harmful stuff to me. At least, that's what the rational side of my mind is saying. The other side is whispering for me to trust him.

Again, *what the hell?*

"What sort of stuff?" I ask, attempting to distract myself from everything going on inside my mind.

He crinkles his nose. "Ogre drama stuff."

"Oh. You mean her ex-boyfriend?"

"She told you about that?"

I nod. "She's told me a lot of things. She's very nice."

"She is sometimes, but she can also be a pain in the ass."

"I'm sure she probably thinks the same thing about you." The words just sort of fall off my tongue.

I'm usually not so snarky, but he brings it out of me.

He appears deeply perplexed by my words, but then he shakes off the look, growing serious.

"How long will it take you to get ready?" he abruptly changes the subject.

"I never agreed to go shopping with you," I reply stubbornly.

"You have to," he says, stepping toward me. "It's important for you to get the stuff that you need so you can fit in here. Because, if you don't fit in, creatures may start wondering about you. Then they might look into you more and find out what you are." He takes another step toward me and lowers his voice, his breath hot against my face. "And if you think my reaction was bad when I found out what you are, imagine having to deal with an entire school of monsters acting that way toward you."

A chill breaks out across my flesh, and I shiver, a clusterfuck of emotions clashing through me the closer he gets.

What the heck is going on with me?

"I understand what you're saying, but I can wait until Harper can go with me." Swallowing down another shiver, I inch away from him. "Because I'm not going with you. I don't trust you."

"And normally, I'd say you're smart for thinking that, but I made a blood promise with Harper that I wouldn't hurt you, so you can trust me now."

Is he telling the truth? I wouldn't know, because I still don't know much about this world.

"I ... I don't know what a blood promise is," I admit.

Sighing, he sticks out his palm. A cut marks his flesh, but it looks like it's already healing. "A blood promise is when two people cut open their palms, make the same promise, and seal it with blood magic. And the promise is unbreakable. The magic makes sure of that." He lowers his hand and meticulously arches his brow. "So, maddening, are you going to be cooperative? Or are you going to spend the entire school year getting tormented because everyone found out what you are?"

As anger courses through my veins, that pull dissolves into nothing—whatever it was to begin with. "Fine. I'll go shopping with you," I snap. "But my name is Haven, not maddening." With that, I spin around and storm out of the room, striding toward the bathroom.

The moment I lock myself in there, all my

confidence crumbles. And so do I ... onto the floor. That pull inside my chest is rising again, tugging hard and begging me to crawl back toward Roman.

Something's wrong.

I think I'm broken.

Then again, I think I've been broken for a very long time.

But this feels worse. Like I shattered and he's holding on to all the pieces.

I think about how yesterday, when we discovered I had wings, how I sensed Harper was keeping something from me. I wonder if this pull has anything to do with that, or if it's just a death angel thing. Whatever it is, I need to turn it off, because the last thing I want is to feel connected to Roman.

HAVEN

Despite the urge to take a long-ass shower just to annoy Roman, I do my best to hurry, telling myself it has nothing to do with the pull. And it might not, since I've never been the kind of person—creature that was okay with going out of their way to annoy someone. Sometimes I wish I was. Maybe then I wouldn't have spent my life being tormented. Who really knows? Maybe it's just me.

About twenty minutes later, I leave the bathroom, dressed, my hair still damp, and only wearing lip gloss and kohl eyeliner for makeup, so yeah, my typical look.

When I step into the living room, Roman is sitting on the sofa, messaging someone on his handheld. He has his head tipped down and seems pretty distracted, not noticing when I enter.

I take a moment to look at him without him being aware that I am. He's gorgeous—that's been a given since day one. There's also a darkness that seems to radiate from him, like a shadowy aura. Again, I noticed that the first time I saw him. Now, though, I can see it clearer. I can also see the cracks in it, like scars and hidden secrets.

He's not as tough as he wants everyone to believe he is.

That thought strikes me out of nowhere and, while I have no idea how, I know it's true.

I'm not sure how long I assess him, but a few minutes tick by. I keep waiting for him to glance up at me, to sense my presence like I so clearly can sense his. But it eventually becomes clear to me that he has no idea I'm here, so I clear my throat to get his attention.

He startles, nearly dropping the handheld, and lets out a string of curses.

I get a bit of satisfaction in knowing I scared him.

"You're jumpy," I note as he quickly turns

over his handheld device so the screen is no longer visible.

Suspicion arises in me. What was he looking at? Clearly, it was something he doesn't want me to see, and that has me extremely worried.

His gaze sweeps across me, and he frowns. "Aren't you going to dry your hair?" he asks, rising to his feet and tucking his handheld into the back pocket of his jeans.

I tuck a strand of my damp hair behind my ear. "Nope."

His frown deepens, and I mentally roll my eyes.

"Is there a problem with my hair being wet? Does it offend you like everything else about me?"

He doesn't answer right away, seemingly conflicted about something.

I remember how I found out yesterday why Roman hates me. Or, well, maddenings. Because one killed his brother. But that doesn't mean he should just hate me. I'm not bad.

I'm not.

No matter how many times I try to convince myself, I can't help thinking about the awful things I've done in the past.

Maybe I am bad.

Maybe he has every right to hate me.

But he doesn't even know me.

"No," he answers, his lips twitching as if he's trying not to smile. Then he grows serious so quickly that I wonder if I imagined it. "But it's cold where we're going."

My brows dip. "How can it be cold? It's barely the beginning of fall."

He studies me closely. "You really don't know anything about these worlds, do you?"

"You already know I don't," I say, wrapping my arms around myself.

"I know, but I thought maybe you were faking your naivety."

"I'm not naïve."

He rolls his eyes. "You're the most naïve creature I've ever met."

The muscles in my jaw pulsate. "Why can't Harper just take me shopping another day? You don't even want to take me anyway."

"How do you know that?" he questions with a cock of his brow.

"Because you hate me," I remind him. "No one wants to spend time with someone they hate, so why don't you just go do whatever the hell it is you do and let Harper take me shopping another day?"

He remains silent for a moment, and I stupidly think perhaps he's considering my offer.

He's not. Not even a little bit.

"Let's go." He strides for the door.

I ball my hands into fists as I stomp after him. "Just because I have wings, doesn't mean we have to spend time together."

He pulls open the door. "That's not why we're spending time together."

"Then, why are we?"

"Because you need to learn more about yourself in preparation for the deadly games." He steps out of the dorm.

"Right, the deadly games." I walk beside him as he heads down the hallway, his boots scuffing against the tiled floor. "Why do you even want me to be on your team? You yourself just said that I'm naïve about this world, and I'm assuming that, in order to participate in these games, you need to be able to use like magic powers and stuff, right?"

"Magic powers?" He cocks a brow, amusement dancing in his eyes. It's a strange look for him.

"Isn't that what they're called?" I ask, unsure what he finds so amusing.

"I guess you could call them that since, technically, that's what they are, but that's not really what anyone calls them."

"So, what do they call them, then?"

He shrugs, stuffing his hands into his pocket "Powers, I guess."

"But that's pretty much what I just said."

"No, you said *magic* powers."

Confusion floods my mind. "All that's different is that I used the word magic."

"I know." He flicks a glance at me, and I can tell he's trying really hard not to smile. It makes me almost want to smile. For a stupid moment, anyway. Then I become aware that that pull has returned, and I question if that might be behind my temporary loss of smiling insanity.

"Magic powers is more like something a young creature would say," he continues to explain, checking the time on his pocket watch. "As we get older, we just refer to them as powers."

"Oh." Maybe I really am naïve. "Well, I didn't know that." I look away and stare ahead, my thoughts drifting to a worry that's been haunting my mind for a few days now. "How am I supposed to blend in here if I don't even know something as simple as the right word choice? I won't even be able to talk to anyone without sounding like a freak." Story of my damn life.

"That's why I'm helping you." He slows to a stop as we arrive at a fork in the hallway.

"So, you're going to teach me how to talk, too?" I question, stopping beside him. "Because that just sounds silly."

"Yeah, it does, since you already know how to talk." A hint of playfulness creeps into his tone.

It sounds weird coming from the person— creature that constantly has dark shadows plaguing his skin and eyes.

"That's not what I meant." I wait for him to choose which side of the hallway we're going down, but he doesn't budge, staring at me confusedly instead.

"Where are we going anyway? I mean, I know Harper said shopping in the city, but where is the city exactly? And how do we get there?"

"That's what I'm trying to decide," he mutters, yanking his gaze from me. Then he eyeballs the two hallways that split apart from each other. "Usually, I fly there."

My eyes nearly bulge out of my head. "*What?*"

He meets my gaze. "Is that fear I smell, maddening?"

I grind my teeth from side to side. "How many times do I have to tell you that my name is Haven?"

He rolls his tongue in his mouth, I think to try to hold back a smile. "You know, usually, when a creature smarts off at me like that, they get punished."

I roll my eyes. "Yeah, well, I really doubt you're going to harm me since you made that blood promise with Harper. And, from what you guys have said, it sounds like you can't hurt me." That's not the truth, though. I have no idea why, but I suddenly *feel* this knowledge that he won't hurt me.

He presses his lips together, his gaze sweeping over me. Then he just stares at me for so long that I start to grow squirmy.

"Why are you looking at me like that?" I ask, uneasiness lacing my tone.

He drags out the silence for a little bit longer

while chewing on his bottom lip. "I'm deciding what to do with you."

As fear and irritation lash through me, I move to leave, even though I'm pretty sure I won't be able to find my way back to the dorm. But, before I can make it more than a step, he sidesteps in front of me. A crackling pause, and then he's suddenly backing me up against the wall.

Those eerie shadows appear, twirling around his skin. Is it a death angel thing? And, if so, will I be able to do it?

"I'm not going to hurt you," he utters, bracing his hand against the wall behind me, his fingers a bit shaky. In fact, I can feel him shaking all over, yet I somehow can't see it. My heart pounds in my chest, seeming to match the rhythm. "Trust me; I can't hurt you even if I wanted to."

I press my back against the brick wall, though that pull pleads with me to lean forward. "Yeah, I know. Because of the blood promise."

"It's not because of the blood promise," he mutters.

As soon as the words leave his lips, his expression plummets, his arms stiffening.

"What is it because of then?" I ask, my eyes searching his.

Why does he look so scared right now?

"Nothing. I didn't mean anything by that." He pushes away from the wall then hurries down the left side of the hallway.

I could walk the other way, leave, try to find my way back to the dorm. And maybe I should. But that pull tells me to go after him. So does my need for the truth.

I need to know what's going on, because something definitely is.

"No, you did mean something by it," I call out as I jog after him. "So tell me."

He swiftly shakes his head. "Just drop it."

"No. I want to know. Because, yesterday, it felt like ... it felt like there was more to this whole me-having-wings thing. Like ... I don't know ... Harper was kind of acting weird."

His gaze glides to me as I reach his side, but then he hastily looks away. "Harper always acts weird."

Maybe he's right. I barely know her. Still ... "It just felt like there was more to me having wings. Like maybe she was keeping something from me. And so are you." And what about this pull I feel toward him? This annoying draw that keeps amplifying with every second that goes by.

"There is more to it. A lot more. " He grinds to a halt in front of a doorway that leads to a spiral stairway. Then he turns toward me, raking his fingers through his hair while letting out a stressed breath.

I realize then that almost every time I've seen him, he's appeared mostly composed. The only exception to this is now and when he saw my wings. Then, he looked like he was freaking out. He kind of looks like he's freaking out right now.

I part my lips to ask him why he looks that way, even though a voice in the back of my mind shouts at me to shut up, to not be concerned about him, but I never get that far, because he talks over me.

"I'm not going to get into that right now." He heads for the stairway.

I rush after him. "Why not?"

"Because now's not the time." He quickens his pace, moving at an inhuman speed.

I assume I can move fast, too. In fact, I read a little bit about myself in that book Harper and I stole from the library. I think it mentioned me having super speed abilities, but I have no clue how to use them. Still, I rush after him, fully planning on confronting him when I reach him.

However, all words are lost when we reach the top of the stairway, which leads to the rooftop.

"I don't ..." My jaw nearly crashes against the ground as I gape at the view while breathing in the fresh air, which strangely smells like snow, despite the lack of it. "This place is ..." My gaze strays upward as I try to process everything I'm seeing.

The glimmering grey sky has two suns; one silver, one lavender. Below, the grass shimmers against the suns' light and midnight blue trees decorate the land. For a while anyway. If I look farther out, I get a glimpse of a city glowing in the distance.

"Wow," I whisper. "This is magical. Like really real magical."

"You really are from the human world, aren't you?" Roman remarks, observing me curiously.

I tear my gaze off the view to look at him. "Yes. Why do you keep questioning that?"

He lifts a shoulder. "Because of what you are. Your kind are known for telling lies."

I look away from him with a heavy sigh. "I know why you hate my kind so much ... because of what happened to your brother. What I don't get, though, is why you're helping me if you're so prejudice against my kind. Why didn't you just tell Harper no when she asked you to help me put my wings back in? Then you wouldn't even have to be standing here with me, questioning everything about me." And I wouldn't have to be here, fighting my conflicting feelings of being near him or running away.

I'm becoming painfully aware that whatever is going on in my body and mind is not of my own free will. It has to be because of magic or something monster-y.

Monster-y? Yeah, I'm glad I said that word inside my head and not aloud.

Roman remains silent for so long that I start to question if he left. When I look to my side, though, he's standing in the same place he was, his shadowy gaze dissecting me.

"How did you find out about my brother?" he asks in a controlled tone, but the shadows are moving wildly across his flesh, as if he's fighting not to unleash them on me. If he can anyway. I'm still not one-hundred percent certain what those shadows do.

When I say nothing, he lowers his voice. "Tell me." Accusation burns in his tone.

I honestly feel bad for him in that moment.

I'm not even sure why. Well, at first, I can't. But then I feel it. A spark of pain. And it's not mine. It's *his*. It's a blinding ache inside my chest that hurts way, way worse than any pain that I've ever felt. It's so powerful that it nearly knocks the breath out of me.

But, that can't be possible, can it? That I can feel his pain. I mean, maybe it could be ... I guess.

It has to be because of whatever's causing that pull.

"I overheard you say it while we were in the cave. And Harper confirmed it later." I give a short, considering pause, debating whether or not to say what's on my mind. On the one hand, he's been a total asshole to me. On the other hand, arguing with him is exhausting. And feeling his pain like this ... it makes me a bit more sympathetic. "Look, I'm really sorry about what happened to your brother—I am. And I get that being around a maddening is hard for you, but ..." I chew on my bottom lip. "I didn't hurt him, and I really wish you'd stop treating me like I did." There, a peace offering. Whether he takes it or not is up to him.

That pain inside my chest withers, like a

fading rose, yet the fragments of the petals remain.

"Have you ever hurt anyone?" he asks, carrying my gaze.

I want to lie, and I plan on lying, but he keeps staring at me in a hypnotic way, and I ...

"I have," I murmur in a daze. "When I was younger, I hurt one of my foster moms with my powers. She was hitting me and yelling at me and hurting me, and I ... I didn't think she was going to stop, and then this darkness crept up inside me ..." I swallow hard. "I didn't mean to do it. And I didn't know what I did at the time. Now, though, I get it."

His pupils completely consume his eyes. "Was that the only time you hurt a person or creature?"

I dazedly shake my head. "Right before I came here, I used my powers to hurt my foster father. Again, though, I didn't know what I was doing."

"Why did you do it?"

"Because he was hurting me again. And ..." Tears sting my eyes. I don't want to say the words aloud, so I bite down on my tongue hard, hoping to stop them. But, even as blood fills my mouth, I can't stop telling him the truth, as if a spell has been cast over me. Part of me wonders if that's exactly what's happening. "He wouldn't stop touching me. He touched me all the time, and I hated it—hated him. And, while I hate myself for hurting him, part of me is glad he's suffering right now in his own madness—or whatever happened to him." I'm panting loudly and tears are streaming down my cheeks.

I want to look away from him, but I can't, bound by a spell that I'm fairly certain he cast on me. Well, either that, or he's using his powers to make me say all these things.

"Is there more?" His voice, which has been steady, is a bit shaky now.

I try to blink the tears away. "No. Not really."

He blinks, and his pupils return to normal, the shadows on his skin dimming. The movement must break the spell because, when I try to force my gaze off him this time, it works.

Sniffling, I hurriedly wipe my eyes with my hands, shame and anger burning in my veins. "What did you do to me?"

"What had to be done," he says without a drop of remorse in his tone.

"Screw you." I reel around, toward the stairway, my hands clenched into fists, preparing to leave, but he snags a hold of the back of my shirt.

"Where the hell are you going? We need to get to the city."

"I'm not going shopping with you." I smack his hand away from my shirt. "I'll wait until Harper can take me. Or I just won't go at all. I don't care." I turn for the stairway again, but he swings around in front of me. I grind my teeth from side to side. "Move out of my way."

He shakes his head, the wind sending strands of his hair into his eyes. "We need to go shopping today. It's important." When I start to shake my head, he sucks in a huge breath. "I'm sorry," he mumbles.

I cross my arms, fury bursting inside me. "For what? For using magic on me to make me spill all my dark secrets? Because I know you did that. I'd never just tell you about ..." Vomit burns my throat as I choke the memories surfacing in my mind.

Hands all over me ...

Touching me ...

I want to hurt him ... my foster father ... I want to make him suffer.

And I did.

I became the monster.

"No, I'm not sorry for doing that. I needed to know the truth about you, or this would never work." He briefly shuts his eyes, his chest rising and crashing as he sucks in a huge breath before he opens his eyes again. His eyes that are now a silvery blue. "I'm sorry you were abused."

That was not what I expected him to say, and the words ... they hit me like a punch to the chest, nearly knocking the wind out of me.

"I wasn't ... I don't ..." I look away from him, taking uneven breaths.

All the scars on my body sear inside me. So do the memories in my mind.

No one has ever said something like that to me. Everyone has always blamed me for all the bad things that happened to me. And deep down, I know part of it has to be my fault. Why else would everyone always say it was?

"It's not your fault," he says, as if reading my mind.

"There's no way you could possibly know that," I mutter, folding my arms around myself.

"Actually, there is."

Dragging my teeth along my bottom lip, I

look at him, expecting him to be smirking at me. He's not. If anything, he looks sad.

"How?" I wonder.

He lifts a shoulder. "Because I can feel it flowing off you right now."

"Feel what flowing off me?"

"The truth."

I swallow hard. "Why couldn't you feel it before? I mean, when you first met me?"

He gives another half-shrug, glancing away for a moment. "Because I didn't know about your wings before." He meets my gaze again. "Now I do, and that ... that makes getting to the truth easier."

"Does me being a death angel connect us or something?" I ask, confused. "Because, just a few minutes ago, I thought I could ... I thought I could feel what you were feeling." If that's what's happening, does that mean I'll be able to feel that with every death angel that I cross paths with?

"It's not because of that," he explains, looking a little scared again, which scares me. I don't know why, other than maybe I'm feeling his emotions again. "It's because of you ... what you are."

"A maddening?" I ask.

He slowly shakes his head, his fear amplifying. "No, that has nothing to do with it," he says evasively.

Even with the pull I feel toward him and his emotions coursing through me, irritation manages to bite at the surface.

"Then, what does it have to do with?" I aim for a demanding tone but miss the mark, probably because I've never been demanding in my life. I wish I was. At least sometimes. "Please just tell me. Because everything is so confusing, and I feel like I'm missing out on something. And I ... Just please tell me what's going on."

I mentally want to kick myself. So much for being demanding. I sound pitiful right now.

Roman must think so, too, since he makes zero effort to answer my pleads.

"You already know a lot about me," I try again. "You used some sort of magic powers on me to get to the truth, so you should tell me the truth."

The corners of his lips spasm as he bites back a smile. I can feel that he thinks something is funny, and as I replay my words, I figure out why.

Because I used the term *magic powers*.

I feel like I'm in school again, getting laughed

at, getting rocks thrown at me, getting kicked, punched, touched. So many things.

I want to leave.

And when tears threaten to pour out of my eyes again, that's exactly what I try to do. A few manage to escape before I can get completely turned around and out of his view.

He sucks in a breath then grabs my arm, turning me back toward him.

"God, will you please just let me go—"

He crashes his lips down on mine.

My eyes snap wide open as I suck in a shaky breath through my nose while lifting my hands to shove him off me. But then he parts my lips with his tongue, and that pull I feel toward him spills down my throat.

Instead of pushing him away, I grasp the bottom of his shirt to keep myself from collapsing as shakiness consumes me.

He must sense my inability to stand, because he puts his hands on my waist to steady me. He's shaking just as badly as I am, though, so I worry we're both about to crumble.

Pull away, Haven. You don't want this.

And part of me knows I don't, but the other part, the one connected to that pull , does. Or maybe it's the loneliness that keeps me from stopping this—whatever this is. Honestly, we're both just standing there like we have no clue what to do, which is the truth for me.

Then, as if something snaps inside him, he kisses me deeply. So deeply I swear he's dragging that pull out of my chest and swallowing it. Maybe that's exactly what he's doing—pulling something out of me. I really don't know. I really don't know anything.

Stupid.

Stupid.

Stupid.

I was called that all the time by my foster families. I think they might've been on to something since I don't pull away. No, stupid me lets him kiss me, lets his hands slide down my back and his fingers tangle through my hair as he tilts my head back. Then he kisses me until I become lightheaded, and I have no choice but to clutch his arms and pull him closer, kissing him back, trying to drink that pull in from him …

"I can't believe she's your fucking wing match," Phoenix says to Roman. "Your other half is a half-maddening! You know that means you can't even torment her anymore. You have to be

nice to her." He flashes him a fanged grin. "Really, really nice to her. But hey, at least she's nice to look at. Maybe you can distract yourself with that when you're fucking her."

"I'm not going to fuck her," Roman bites out, rage burning through his body. "Just because she's my wing match, doesn't mean I'm going to be with her. I could never be with her. Not like that. It disgusts me just thinking about it."

"You say that now"—Phoenix grins as he leans back against the sofa and tucks his hands behind his head—"but we'll see when the wing match magic really kicks in. Depending on how linked you guys become, it could take over."

"It'll never come to that," Roman growls. "Because my hatred for her kind will always be stronger."

"Will it?" Phoenix questions. "Because I thought I saw something different in your eyes, other than hate, when you saw those pretty wings sprouting out of her back."

Lust pounds inside Roman as he remembers what I looked like with my wings, but I can also feel how much he doesn't want to feel that way.

How much he doesn't want to feel that way toward me.

I jerk back, breaking the kiss and gasping for air. Roman is breathing just as heavily as he opens his eyes, his gaze wild as he stares at me. His chest is rising and crashing, and so many emotions are coursing through him that I can't tell what he's feeling.

And I don't really care.

I shove him back, and he surprisingly stumbles.

"What the heck's a wing match?" I remember Harper saying something about it the other day. I just can't recall what it is.

His eyes fleetingly widen, but he promptly collects himself. "What're you talking about?"

"Don't play dumb with me. I saw ... I ..." I trail off, trying to figure out what just happened. I saw him talking to Phoenix, but it was like I was hovering in the shadows, as if I was eavesdropping on a memory. "What game are you playing? Some stupid monster mindfuck? Because, if so, you're doing a damn good job!" He is, because I'm all riled up and can't think clearly.

Maybe this is what he wanted the entire time.

"You saw what?" he hedges with a curious expression, ignoring my remark.

"I saw you talking to Phoenix. Well, I think I saw …" I yank my fingers through my hair as confusion pounds through my body. "This is … This is mad. I'm mad. I really am." I shake my head, lowering my hand to my side and glaring at him. Whether I'm mad or not is beside the point right now. "What's a wing match?"

His eyes search mine, and then he steps toward me. When I step back, he blows out an exasperated sigh.

"I'm not going to hurt you."

I take another step back. "What's a wing match?"

A look of contemplation crosses his face. "I'll tell you, but only if you explain to me what the heck just happened while I was kissing you."

At the mention of the kiss, my lips begin to tingle. I absentmindedly reach up to touch them, and his gaze tracks the movement, his eyes locking on my lips. The longer he stares at them, the faster my heart beats. And when he leans in to kiss me again, I almost let him. But then I snap back to reality and place a hand on his chest, stopping him.

"What's a wing match?" I repeat. A lot of the

confidence has left my voice and is replaced by … want?

No, that can't be right.

His heart slams against my palm as he locks gazes with me. "It's like … It means our wings were woven from the same wing weaver."

Right. I remember now that Harper had mentioned something like that.

"It's kind of like a soulmate. Except, when a death angel finds their wing match, they can combine their powers and become super powerful. I think it has to do with their feathers being laced with magic belonging to the same wing weaver."

Soulmate? The word smacks me hard across the face.

"No." I shake my head as I back away from him. "We're not soulmates."

"No, we're not," he agrees, watching me closely. "We're wing matches, which is more powerful than a soulmate." He's the portrait of indifference, which pisses me off.

"You don't even like me!" I snap, reality washing over me. "It's some magic thing … That's why you kissed me … That's why I let my first kiss happen with you …" I bite down on my tongue to stop myself from rambling.

He looks at me with pity. "That was your first kiss?"

"That wasn't stolen from me, yeah." I shake my head, trying to clear that pull from my body that seems to be keeping me here with him.

I want to run. Leave. Never look at him. But I can't get my feet to cooperate.

"I'm sorry," he says quietly.

I'm not sure if he's saying he's sorry for kissing me or because people kissed me all the time without my permission. Whatever the reason, I don't care. All I can see is that disgust in his eyes from the memory I saw of him talking to Phoenix.

"I ..." He starts to say something then thinks better of it. "What happened while I was kissing you? What did you see?"

"How do you know I saw anything?"

"Because you started to say that you did then stopped yourself."

I scratch my wrist, not wanting to tell him, but it's like he pulls the words out of my mouth. "I saw what I think is a memory of yours, of when you were talking to him about me being your wing match." The image of the disgust on his face floods my mind.

So does the kiss we just shared.

My first real kiss that I chose to have, and it was with someone who didn't even really want to kiss me.

More than ready to leave, I move to swing around him, but he reaches to stop me. This time, I'm ready, though, and skitter back, but then I end up tripping over my shoelaces.

My skitter turns into a stumble, and then I'm suddenly falling.

Off the damn roof.

For the briefest moment, I'm relieved it's all over.

Relieved that I no longer have to worry about getting hurt anymore.

I honestly thought I'd hesitate when she starts to fall off the roof. I thought that I'd let her fall, slam against the ground, and break a few bones. But I don't hesitate for even a second and, deep down, I'm aware it has nothing to do with the wing match.

I opened Pandora's box when I used the magic to drag the truth from her pretty lips. The truth about what kind of a monster she really is. And it turns out that she's a completely broken one. One of the most broken I've ever met. Just like me, Ollie, and Phoenix. It's part of the reason me and the guys connected, why we're friends. And now, here I am, about to connect with a maddening who's my wing match.

Destiny is a sick freak of nature. It really is, I think to myself as I rip off my shirt, leap off the ledge, and let my wings snap out of my back. Then I soar downward, straight at Haven, moving quicker than a monster can fall.

I reach her just in time, looping my arms around her. A slamming second of a heartbeat later, my feet touch the ground with her cradled in my arms.

She blinks up at me, her eyes wide and filled with ... disappointment?

That's when I feel it—what she feels. I know it's the wing match magic doing it. It still surprises me, though.

Wing match magic works a bit differently for all death angels. Sometimes the magic works strongly, forming a deeply intricate connection. Most often, though, it only runs as deep as skin surface. I assumed that's the kind of connection I'd have with Haven. It's not. I can tell by the way I feel everything she feels, and by the way I was drawn to kiss her. However, the magic was only part of the driving force behind that kiss. The other part lay inside those fucking tears in her eyes.

She's so broken. Nothing like the maddenings that I've met and heard about. I can see it in her eyes. Can feel it consuming her veins.

She's disappointed because part of her wanted to crash against the ground, didn't want me to catch her. I don't know what to do with that, because I've fucking felt that before. That hopeless despair that you'd do almost anything to get rid of. I felt it the most right after my brother died.

Right after a maddening killed him.

A maddening, just like her.

I want to hate her. I want to look her in the eyes and feel that hate I felt when I first found out what she was. The truth is, though, that while I hate the idea of her, I don't hate her. I don't know her well enough to hate her. I just didn't—wouldn't—admit that to myself, because it made me feel like I was betraying my brother.

My brother wouldn't want me to, either. Hate Haven, I mean. Deep down, I know that. He was never like our parents—full of hate and prejudice, becoming the definition of the magic that pollutes our veins. I think he's the only reason I was so nice and gentle when I was younger. Then he died, and all that was left was my father's harsh words and punishments. Just coldness and darkness and despair. That's all I am anymore. And I was okay with that. I thought so, anyway. Now this wing match is thawing my cold, dead veins.

Death angels aren't supposed to feel warm. Our magic is derived from death itself. We are linked to the dead. Those shadows that appear on my skin are the magic of the dead, the essence of the souls that are trapped in the Underworld. Maddenings and death angels are alike like that. But, where death angels simply channel their energy from souls, maddenings steal the energy of the living and sentence the souls to endure torture in the Underworld.

That's why I thought I hated Haven the moment I discovered what she was. Thought being the keyword. And then I found out about her past, and now I have no clue how I think I should feel anymore.

I am completely and utterly confused, and I hate it.

I glance down at her in my arms, debating whether or not to set her down. She's clutching on to me for dear life, like she's afraid I'm going to do just that.

"Are you okay?" I decide to start there.

She peers around. "Yeah, I ..." She grimaces. "One of my foster mom's used to tell me all the time that, if I didn't start tying my laces, I was going to trip and fall. I guess she was right. I just didn't think it'd be that dramatic of a fall."

My lips quirk at that.

So do hers. Then she presses them together, erasing the smile.

I become aware that I don't think I've seen her smile much.

Like I'm one to talk.

"I didn't think you'd catch me," she admits. "I guess that wing match magic does have its perks." She acts grateful, but inside, I can tell she's only partly grateful. The other part of her is sad.

Like when I saw her cry, I feel the urge to touch her again. To kiss her. To give in to that pull I feel humming between us. I may have done just that, but then she starts staring at my wings in awe then reaches up and touches one.

"They look a lot like mine, but not exactly the same." She brushes her finger along another feather.

I resist a shiver, but fuck, my whole body craves to convulse. I've never felt anything like it.

It must be the wing match magic. It has to be.

"Why do my feathers have an iridescent glimmer to them and yours has a red tint"—she looks at me, still playing with the tips of my feathers—"if our feathers were woven by the same wing weaver or whatever it's called?"

"Yeah, that's what they're called," I tell her shakily. I want to sound more composed and hate that I don't, but she keeps touching my wings and I keep losing control over my body. "And I'm guessing ours are a little different because you're only part death angel."

"So, the magic between us isn't as strong?" With the tips of her fingers, she traces the side of my wing.

I stiffly shake my head. "No, it definitely is."

A crease forms between her brows. "Why are you so tense suddenly?"

"Because ..." I release an unsteady breath as she continues fondling my wing. "Because you keep touching my feathers, and it's making me feel like I'm about to jump out of my skin."

"Oh." She jerks back. "Oh my God, I'm so sorry. I didn't even realize I was doing that." Her cheeks tint pink.

Oh my hell, if I thought her fondling my

wings was bad, it's nothing compared to that blush.

As my entire body convulses, I set her down on the ground as gently as I can.

While I'm certain she has no clue what's going on, she doesn't ask, taking a step back from me. I take a step back, too, despite how much I want to walk forward and pick her up again.

Silence stretches between us as I stare at her openly while she keeps sneaking glances up at me but mostly focuses on the ground. Her uneasiness stirs in the air.

She's partly afraid of me, at least where the magic isn't controlling her emotions. I should be grateful for that. It's what I wanted. Or, at least I thought I wanted. But that was before …

Before what, Roman? Before you found out she was your wing match? Before the wing match magic decided to turn on? Before you found out how broken she is?

Before you lost control over what you've been trying to be?

A cold, dead shell who can never hurt again.

Gods, I'm so confused.

"I didn't just catch you because of the magic," I admit. "I caught you because I didn't want you to ... to get hurt." *What the hell am I doing?* "Not that it'd hurt for very long. Maddenings and death angels are extremely strong. However, it would've hurt for a bit. You may have even broken a few bones. Those would've healed quickly, though."

"Oh." A pucker forms between her brows as she tucks a strand of hair behind her ear. "You know, while I was falling, I didn't even think about that. I thought I was going to die. I guess I'm used to thinking I'm human."

Us monsters consider humans fragile. While Haven may be one of the most powerful monsters to ever exist, I think she might be almost as fragile as a human. At least in the position she is now—utterly clueless about everything. She has to rely on Harper and me to guide her through this.

She's lucky Harper is a good creature. For the most part, anyway. And she's lucky she turned out to be a death angel and my wing match, because I'm not sure I could've seen past her breed had it not been for those wings snapping out of her back. They snapped me out of my current form of who I am and briefly sent me back to the past when I was nicer.

And now I'm unsure who I'm supposed to be.

So much for being a good guide.

"You'll get used to it eventually," I try to assure her.

"I don't know about that. All of this is so weird." She angles her head to the side and stares up at the sky. "Even the sky looks different here. In the human world, it's blue during the day, and it has one sun that looks like a giant fireball."

I'll admit, it's kind of fascinating to watch her take everything in with such awe.

"Wait until you see the night sky. Although, it's not nearly as pretty as the winter sky."

She blinks at me. "Winter sky?"

"Did the human world not have one of those?"

She shakes her head, strands of her long, dark hair blowing into her face. "No. We had the night sky and the day sky. And the cloudy sky. That's about it."

"So no summer sky? Spring? Autumn? Monster Hollow Day?" I jot off all the different skies I can think of, and she shakes her head.

"Monster Hollow Day? What's that?" she asks, curiosity sparkling in her eyes.

I've called her naïve a handful of times, and she is. Right now, I think it's kind of adorable. Not that I'll divulge that aloud. Besides, it's dangerous for her to be so clueless about everything. She needs training. Hardcore training. And before everyone shows up at the academy.

I worry that students will be arriving soon. More than likely, they'll start trickling in tonight.

Why do I get the feeling this is going to end badly?

And why does the idea that it will make my chest constrict?

"Are you okay?" she asks. "You feel like you're ... I don't know, distraught or something." She nibbles on her bottom lip. "What is that connection anyway? I mean, why can I feel what you're feeling?"

I give a half-shrug. "Because we're wing matches."

"Oh ... What else will happen between us?"

"I'm not sure."

"You don't know everything about this?" That seems to surprise her.

I shake my head. "I don't know everything about wing matches and, to be honest, there's not really a way to find out everything about them since every wing match is different."

"Oh ... Can you ...? You know what? Never mind." She looks up at the sky again, but only to avoid eye contact with me.

"What is it?" I ask as the glittering grass crunches beneath my feet. When she looks at me dubiously, I add, "Go ahead and ask. I need to answer as many of your questions as possible so you'll know as much as possible and blend in as much as possible."

She cracks a small smile. "That's a lot of possibles."

"Yeah, it definitely is," I agree, almost smiling myself. "But the possibles are important."

She nods, puzzlement continuing to mask her features. "I was just going to ask if you can feel what I'm feeling, too. And can you ...? Can you see any of my memories?" Worry creeps into her eyes then dissipates when I shake my head.

"No to the memories part." Although, I have a feeling that if she has the power to do that to me, then I have the power to do that to her, since I know for a fact that ability isn't from maddening or death angel power. "Yes to the feelings."

"Oh." Her lips curve downward. "When have you?"

"A couple of times just barely on the roof." I pause. "And while you were falling. I saw and felt ... your disappointment."

Her throat muscles work as she swallows hard. "I don't ..." Shame floods her cheeks, and she quickly tips her head down.

"It's okay." Driven by a force I still can't comprehend, I reach forward and brush my fingers across her hand. Then I try not to take it personally when she jolts and steps back from me, wrapping her arms around herself.

"Why are you being so nice to me now?" she mutters, refusing to meet my gaze. "It's because of the match thing, isn't it?"

"I'm honestly not sure," I admit. "I used to be a nicer creature, but then shit happened and that niceness died with it."

Now I'm the one to look away as painful memories stir inside me. Memories of the last day I ever saw my brother alive.

I can feel the darkness swelling inside.

"What are those shadow things on your skin?" she asks quietly.

I'm relieved by the distraction and look at her, opening my mouth. "I—"

A tree branch snaps from somewhere close by and, with instincts I wasn't aware I possessed, I swing around in front of Haven protectively as I reach for my dagger. Then I relax when I spot Ollie strolling out of the trees, still wearing the all-black outfit he had on when I saw him in the early hours of morning. Although, when I see the grin on his face, my relief dissipates.

I expect him to tease the hell out of me for the fact that I just tried to protect a maddening, but by the time he reaches us, his smile has faded.

"Where are you going?" he asks as he slows to a stop in front of us.

"I made a deal with your sister," I inform him, "which requires me to take Haven shopping." When amusement glitters in his eyes, I glare at him. "Don't even say it."

He elevates his hands in front of him. "I didn't say a word."

I notice he has sparkling iridescent magic coating his palms.

What in the faeries? Where has he been?

Before I can ask, he leans around me to catch Haven's eye. "Hello, Haven. You don't have to hide behind my friend. I'm not going to hurt you."

I hear Haven mutter something under her breath. Then she steps out from behind me.

"Hi," Ollie says with a smile.

She gives him a small wave then folds her arms around herself and seals her lips together, apprehension flowing off her.

I can't really blame her. The last time she saw Ollie and me together, we were in that cave.

Ollie studies her for a beat before looking at me. If he was Phoenix, he would've teased Haven a bit for being so quiet. But Ollie is fairly quiet himself. Well, more quiet than Phoenix.

"I'm actually glad I ran into you," he tells me. "Can I talk to you before you take off? Back in our dorm?"

I glance at the time on my pocket watch. "It's already getting pretty late. Can't it wait until we get back?"

He gives me *the look*, the one we give each other when we have something extremely important to say but don't want to say it aloud.

"Okay, yeah, fine." I turn toward Haven.

"Can I drop you off back at your dorm for a bit, and then come pick you back up?"

I'm well-aware that Ollie is watching us closely and is probably curious as to why I'm being so polite.

She shrugs, fiddling with a leather band on her wrist. "You're the one who knows more about this time thing than I do. Honestly, Harper tried to explain it to me, but it confused the hell out of me."

"It'll get easier the longer you're here," I try to assure her when, honestly, I don't know. I was raised in this world, so everything feels natural to me. "I'll make sure we have enough time."

She nods. "Okay."

That's when I feel it.

In that moment, she trusts me.

And I don't know what to do with that.

Because sometimes I don't even trust myself.

ROMAN

After I drop Haven off at her dorm room, Ollie and I go back to ours.

Phoenix is lying down on the sofa when we walk in, on the verge of falling asleep.

"So," Ollie says the moment we get the door shut, "that whole wing match thing seems to be going well."

Phoenix sits up, now wide awake, his eyes sparkling with intrigue. "Why? What happened?"

Ollie doesn't answer him, simply looking at me.

I wonder how much of what happened between Haven and me he saw. How long was he out in those trees? Better yet, what was he doing out there?

"What were you even doing in the woods?" I ask in an obvious subject change.

Ollie stares at me for a moment before letting it drop and wandering toward the sofa. "I went into the city this morning."

I move over to the bar to pour myself a drink. "To do what?"

When he doesn't answer, I glance over my shoulder and catch him and Phoenix trading a look.

As frustration bursts through me, I down the drink then turn toward them. "This whole secretive thing is already getting annoying."

Phoenix cocks a brow at me. "Well, your avoidance in telling us what happened between you and Haven is annoying, as well."

He has me there.

"Whatever." Letting the subject drop, I push away from the bar and plop down in a chair. "So, what did you need to talk to me about?" I ask Ollie. "Because I'm on a time crunch."

"Why?" Phoenix asks as he reaches for a goblet of blood that's on the table.

"Because he's taking Haven shopping," Ollie tells him as he reaches into his jacket pocket.

I give him a dirty look as Phoenix busts up laughing.

"What the hell? For reals?" he asks me through his laughter.

"It was part of the deal I made with Harper," I explain with a heavy sigh. "She couldn't take her, and Haven needs new stuff to help her blend."

"Why couldn't my sister take her?" Ollie asks as he pulls his hand out of his pocket.

I shrug. "She had a meeting with a professor she's assisting for."

A crinkle forms at his brows. "That's weird. I didn't even know she was assisting this year." He sinks into silence for a second before shaking his head. Then he shows me something in his hand. "This is why I snuck into the city this morning."

Laying in his palm is the feather from Haven's wing that I took.

Underneath the light, it shimmers iridescent, and I realize it matches the magic coating Ollie's palms.

"Did you take this from my room?" I ask as I pluck the feather from his hand.

"Sorry," he apologizes. "But there was something bugging me about her feathers, and I wanted to look into it without bringing you into it. However, what I found out ... you need to know."

Phoenix scoots forward on the sofa. "What did you find out?"

Ollie glances between the two of us. "Well, I thought it was strange that Haven's wings had an iridescent glow when she's Roman's wing match and his are tinted red."

"But she's only half death angel," I point out. "It could be from her maddening blood."

"Yeah, but the iridescent glow looks extremely similar to the magic of a rare species of dark fey," he explains cautiously. "So, I went to visit a magic reader to see what they could tell me about it. And don't get worked up about it. It's a creature I trust."

He reads me like an open book. I was about to freak out that he risked someone else finding out about Haven when no one can know about her until we find out more about her.

"So, what did you find out?" I ask, tracing the edge of the feather in my hand.

He takes deep breath then lets it out. "That feather has violet dark fey magic in it."

"Violet dark fey magic?" I question. "I thought that kind of fey were extinct."

"So did I." Ollie reclines back in the seat. "But clearly, Haven has a little bit of it in her blood."

"How?" Phoenix asks, gaping at him. "How can she be maddening, death angel, and violet dark fey?"

"Yeah, that's what I'd like to know," I mumble.

This is bad.

Really, really bad.

It was already dangerous enough that Haven was a maddening/death angel hybrid. But now she's also part violet dark fey, a species that was supposed to be extinct.

"No one can find out about this until we discover more," I inform them with a pressing look. "Not even Harper."

"I completely agree with you," Ollie assures me.

I look at Phoenix for confirmation, and he nods.

"I want to win the deadly games, so I'll keep quiet," he says.

His reason should be mine as well, but it's not.

The truth is that I want to protect Haven. With her past being such a mystery, however. I'm not sure how. I'll figure it out, though.

The wing match magic and the old Roman will make sure of that.

HARPER

I'M LYING, AND I HATE IT. HOWEVER, I DON'T want to mention anything until I find out for sure what's going on. I blame it on being raised by faeries. We're tricky creatures, which leads to a lot of distrust. So, when Jude informed us that an anonymous sponsor gave Haven a large sum of money, I had to look into it.

I never really had an appointment with my professor. I snuck off to meet up with my ex-boyfriend, Trystan. And yes, he's the sexy ogre. A sexy ogre that is extremely good at digging up secrets, like, say, magical money transactions that are supposedly untraceable.

I know I was supposed to go shopping with Haven today, but this was more pressing.

Besides, the city can be dangerous and, while I'm pretty powerful, Roman is definitely more so. And even though I made a big deal about not trusting him with Haven, I do—she's his wing match. He may try to pretend like it doesn't mean anything, but it does. He won't hurt her and, truthfully, I have this intuition that he may end up liking her despite all the odds. At least, if the old Roman still exists, the one before his brother died. That Roman was kind and gentle, and so is Haven. Honestly, they could be perfect for each other if they can get past their issues.

"All right, so here's what I found out," Trystan says as he sets down his handheld. "The transaction came from the world of Vines and Thorns."

"Vines and Thorns?" That's weird. The only creatures that are rich there are the royal family. Other than that, the place is quite poverty-stricken. "Well, can you see who sent it?"

He shakes his head, strands of his blond hair falling into his eyes. "Sorry, Har, but whoever set up that account put some hardcore magic sealing on the files. I was lucky to even be able to track it back to the world the transaction came from."

Great. This doesn't help much.

Then again, I'm not even sure what I'm looking for.

"I know you said you can't tell me what this is about," Trystan says, "but, if you could give me a little bit more details, I might be able to help."

I shake my head. "Sorry, but I can't."

He eyes me over. "It's not like you to be so secretive."

He's completely wrong. I'm a very secretive creature. I just play the role of being an open book because that's what I was taught to do.

Never let anyone in, Harper, my grandma once told me. *They'll crush you if you do.*

"Thanks for your help." I rise to my feet.

"Yeah, okay," Trystan mutters, probably feeling used.

I feel bad, but I have more important things to tend to. Like trying to find out who in the hell would send Haven money from the world of Thorn and Vines.

After I leave Trystan's room, I wander into the library to get a book on the world. Then I sit down and start skimming through the pages. A few compass rotation clicks later, I read something interesting.

Apparently, a long, long time ago, many

maddenings resided on the world of Thorns and Vines. But, like everywhere else, they were weeded out because of fear. Some believe, though, that one of the princesses helped some maddenings go into hiding.

I'm unsure if that means anything, but I do find it a bit unnerving.

What if whoever sent the money knows what Haven is? And if they do, what are they planning to do with her?

ABOUT THE AUTHOR

Jessica Sorensen is a *New York Times* and *USA Today* bestselling author who lives in the snowy mountains of Wyoming. When she's not writing, she spends her time reading and hanging out with her family.

For information: jessicasorensen.com

Monster Academy for the Magical Series:

Monster Academy for the Magical

Monster Academy for the Magical: The Deadly Four

Untitled (coming soon)

Enchanted Chaos Series:

Enchanted Chaos

Shimmering Chaos

Iridescent Chaos

Entangled Chaos (coming soon)

Capturing Magic:

Chasing Wishes

Chasing Magic

Untitled (coming soon)

Chasing Hadley Harlyton:

Chasing Hadley

Falling for Hadley

Holding onto Hadley

Untitled (coming soon)

Cursed Hadley:

Cursed Hadley

Enchanting Hadley (coming soon)

Tangled Realms:

Forever Violet

Untitled (coming soon)

Curse of the Vampire Queen:

Tempting Raven

Enchanting Raven

Alluring Raven

Untitled (coming soon)

Unraveling You Series:

Unraveling You

Raveling You

Awakening You

Inspiring You

Every Single Breath

Untitled (coming soon)

<u>Unexpected Series:</u>

The Unexpected Complications of Revenge

Untitled (coming soon)

<u>Shadow Cove Series:</u>

What Lies in the Darkness

What Lies in the Dark

Untitled (coming soon)

<u>Mystic Willow Bay Series:</u>

The Secret Life of a Witch

Broken Magic

Untitled (coming soon)

<u>Standalones:</u>

The Forgotten Girl

<u>The Honeyton Series:</u>

The Illusion of Annabella

Untitled (coming soon)

<u>Rebels & Misfits Series:</u>

Confessions of a Kleptomaniac

Rules of a Rebel and a Shy Girl

Secrets We Buried

Untitled (coming soon)

The Fareland Society:

Opposite of Ordinary

Untitled (coming soon)

Broken City Series:

Nameless

Forsaken

Oblivion

Forbidden (coming soon)

Guardian Academy Series:

Entranced

Entangled

Enchanted

The Forest of Shadow & Bone

Entice

Charmed

Untitled (coming soon)

Lila and Ethan: Forever and Always

Ella and Micha: Infinitely and Always

Untitled (coming soon)

The Shattered Promises Series:

Shattered Promises

Fractured Souls

Unbroken

Broken Visions

Scattered Ashes

Breaking Nova Series:

Breaking Nova

Saving Quinton

Delilah: The Making of Red

Nova and Quinton: No Regrets

Tristan: Finding Hope

Wreck Me

Ruin Me

The Fallen Star Series:

The Fallen Star

The Underworld

The Vision

The Promise

The Lost Soul

The Evanescence

The Mist of Starts (coming soon)

The Darkness Falls Series:

Darkness Falls

Darkness Breaks

Darkness Fades

The Death Collectors Series (NA and YA):

Ember X and Ember

Cinder X and Cinder

Spark X and Spark

Unbeautiful Series:

Unbeautiful

Untamed

9 781939 045478